The Hostage Princess
NOVEL

The Hostage Princess

Ryder Windham

SCHOLASTIC INC.

New York • Toronto • London • Auckland • Sydney
Mexico City • New Delhi • Hong Kong • Buenos Aires

ISBN 0-439-45881-1

12 11 10 9 8 7 6 5 4 3 2 1   2 3 4 5 6 7/0

Printed in the U.S.A.
First Scholastic printing, December 2002

The Hostage Princess

INTRODUCTION

When a mysterious, droid-piloted starship threatened to wreak havoc on the planet Fondor, Jedi Knight Obi-Wan Kenobi and his apprentice, Anakin Skywalker, intervened and destroyed the ship. Unbeknownst to the two Jedi, the ship—a replica of a legendary craft named the *Sun Runner*—had been constructed by Groodo the Hutt, a competitive starship manufacturer from the planet Esseles, who was scheming to put Fondor's orbital starship yards out of business. After the replica's destruction, Groodo was summoned to the Fondor system by his unlikely co-conspirator, Senator Rodd of Fondor.

Despite the Jedi victory, Obi-Wan and Anakin became separated during their mission, and Anakin was stranded on Fondor's jungle-covered moon, Nallastia. Jedi Knight Bultar Swan was prepared to accompany Obi-Wan to Nallastia, but Obi-Wan had a feeling they might require backup, so they transmitted a message to the Jedi Council and requested reinforcements.

Before any additional Jedi could reach the Fondor system, Obi-Wan and Bultar tracked Anakin to a Nallastian fortress, the stronghold of the Skull Queen. There, Anakin made a desperate effort to rescue two zoologists who had been wrongly accused of poaching, and thus were captured and sentenced to death by Princess Calvaria. To prevent the zoologists from being crushed by a condensing force field, the Jedi had to recover the Lost Stars of

Nallastia, three ancient power gems with force-field-disabling properties. The Jedi were aided by the Nallastian leader, Margravine Quenelle, also known as the Skull Queen, mother of Princess Calvaria.

After the zoologists were rescued, an exhausted Anakin tried to get some rest at the Skull Queen's fortress while Obi-Wan and Bultar attended a banquet with the Nallastians. During the meal, the Skull Queen unexpectedly announced she had decided to marry Obi-Wan. This shocking declaration was immediately followed by another, as Princess Calvaria insisted that *she* would wed Obi-Wan...

CHAPTER ONE

"*You* wish to marry Obi-Wan Kenobi?" the Skull Queen asked her daughter.

"It is not only my wish, but my destiny," Princess Calvaria responded from the other side of the banquet table. In stunned silence, the seated figures of Obi-Wan, Bultar Swan, and two dozen Nallastian warriors watched the Skull Queen and Calvaria.

"Destiny?" the Skull Queen gasped. "Whatever are you prattling about?"

Calvaria answered, "Of Nallastia's power gems, it is written:

> '*He who finds the stars of yore*
> *Where others fear to tread,*
> *Will also find his heart is for*
> *Calvaria, and they will wed.*'"

The Skull Queen burst out laughing. "And where is *that* written?" she snickered. "In your own fluff-filled diary?"

Calvaria replied, "As a royal member of the Skull Clan, my journal is valid scripture. And I trust with my soul that the words are true." She turned and beamed at the dumbfounded Obi-Wan, who tried not to squirm in his chair.

Obi-Wan said, "If I may point out—"

Glaring at Calvaria, the Skull Queen interrupted, "Perhaps you have forgotten, my darling daughter, that you are betrothed to Prince Alto of the Raptor Clan, and that your wedding is tomorrow?"

Obi-Wan and Bultar swapped glances. This was

the first time they had heard about Princess Calvaria's wedding.

"I have not forgotten anything!" Calvaria snapped. "I refuse to marry an odorous nest-dweller."

"Who are you to judge the Raptor Clan?" asked the Skull Queen. "You haven't even *met* Prince Alto."

"But I know he cannot be much of a man," Calvaria said. "By recovering the Lost Stars, Obi-Wan has proved he is the greatest warrior to ever walk on our world. His rightful place is by my side."

"He has already chosen me," said the Skull Queen. "He took my hand in the Cavern of Screaming Skulls."

Bultar looked at Obi-Wan, who reluctantly admitted under his breath, "Only to guide her through a dizzying hall of mirrors."

The Skull Queen smiled sweetly at Obi-Wan. "Before you, the last man to hold my hand was my late husband."

"And look where that got him!" Calvaria snarled at her mother.

"Insolent whelp!" countered the Skull Queen.

"Doddering battle-axe!"

"Insufferable appendage!"

"Fortress-wrecker!"

"Please," Obi-Wan said, rising to his feet. "I am unfamiliar with your customs regarding courtship and matrimony, and I regret if I have done anything to mislead either of you. But you must understand that I am…not available. I am a Jedi. And as such, my loyalty is to the Jedi Order."

"You cannot marry?" asked the Skull Queen.

"That is correct."

With a knowing smile, the Skull Queen said, "Ah, but I have heard of a Cerean Jedi Master named Ki-Adi-Mundi. Is he not married?"

Obi-Wan looked to Bultar Swan, who could plainly see that her fellow Jedi Knight did not want to answer any more of the Skull Queen's questions. Remaining seated, Bultar leaned forward in her chair and said, "Because of the low birthrate of Cereans, Master Ki-Adi-Mundi is exempt from the Jedi edict that discourages marriage."

The Skull Queen asked, "And has he been married long?"

"He has been with his wives for many years," Bultar replied truthfully.

"*Wives*?" Calvaria said, surprised. "How many does he have?"

"Two," Bultar said. "As I said, the Cerean birthrate is very low, and they—"

Before Bultar could finish, Calvaria exploded, "I *refuse* to share Obi-Wan with another!"

"That won't be a problem," said the Skull Queen, "since he won't be yours at all!" Turning to Obi-Wan, she said, "So Jedi *can* marry. Unless you forgot, your edicts are somewhat flexible; it seems you were not entirely truthful."

"I am not a Cerean," Obi-Wan replied. "I stand by my words."

"Now, *really*, Obi-Wan," interrupted the Skull Queen. "I appreciate your attempt to spare Calvaria embarrassment in front of all who are gathered but, if we are to be wife and husband, you must be more honest with me."

Calvaria exclaimed, "It is you who should be embarrassed, Mother. Obi-Wan and I will not tolerate your—"

"Stop!" Obi-Wan said, louder than he had intended. He took a deep breath and felt a sharp pain. In the Cavern of Screaming Skulls, he had broken two ribs, and they had not yet completely healed. Calming himself, he continued, "I believe I have made myself clear. I will *not* be marrying *anyone*."

Calvaria exchanged a menacing stare with her mother, then said, "Duel in one hour? Loser to relinquish all claims to Obi-Wan's heart?"

"Accepted," the Skull Queen answered.

Obi-Wan raised his eyebrows. "Duel?"

Ignoring Obi-Wan, the Skull Queen said, "After I defeat you in combat, Calvaria, you will prepare for your wedding to Prince Alto."

"You won't defeat me, Mother," Calvaria answered. "And Prince Alto can go marry a mud-eating venrap." Looking to Obi-Wan, she said, "I shall prove myself worthy of your affections." Before the flabbergasted Obi-Wan could respond, Calvaria turned and left the banquet room.

"This has gone too far," Obi-Wan said to the Skull Queen. "I insist you call off the duel at once."

"Since Calvaria challenged me, only she can call it off," the Skull Queen replied. "But you can dismiss her claim to love you, Obi-Wan. She is angry with me because I arranged her marriage to Prince Alto without her consent. Their marriage is necessary to maintain peace between the Raptor Clan and our own Skull Clan. Calvaria will learn to love Alto. You need not worry about her."

"I am not worried about either you or Calvaria," Obi-Wan stated. "I am troubled by the way you two are more willing to fight than listen to each other, let alone listen to me."

A Nallastian guard entered the banquet hall and announced, "A Republic Cruiser has requested permission to land."

"It must be carrying our reinforcements," Bultar said.

The Skull Queen asked, "Reinforcements for what?"

Obi-Wan said, "Although the replica of the *Sun Runner* was destroyed, I sense the danger is not over. If not here, then on Fondor. We may require assistance."

"Permission is granted," the Skull Queen said to the guard. "Direct the cruiser to the fortress's landing field."

Obi-Wan exhaled a sigh of relief. He could hardly wait to leave Nallastia.

As the guard left the hall, the Skull Queen turned to Obi-Wan and said, "It would please me if you remained until my fight with Calvaria is over. Now, if you'll excuse me, I must prepare for the duel." The Skull Queen clapped her hands twice. All the Nallastian warriors rose from the table and followed their leader out of the hall, leaving Obi-Wan and Bultar alone at the table.

Bultar said, "I think the Skull Queen and her daughter like you."

Obi-Wan scowled. "That isn't funny."

"On a more serious note, we ran into trouble here, but we handled it. Do you really think we still need reinforcements?"

"Yes," Obi-Wan said. "At least, I believe we will. Ever since we were on the space station in orbit around Fondor, I've felt a sense of dread. Even after we found the power gems and rescued the zoologists, I still had a feeling that the Fondor system is being threatened by sinister forces."

"And you suspect Senator Rodd is somehow involved?"

"Call it a hunch," Obi-Wan said. "Do you know where Anakin's room is?"

"Yes. Shall I wake him?"

"Please. Then bring him to the landing field."

"Too bad he was so exhausted," Bultar commented. "I'm sure he'll be sorry he wasn't present for our dinner conversation with the Nallastians. Will we be staying for the duel?"

Obi-Wan sighed. "I'll meet you at the landing field."

CHAPTER TWO

Anakin lay sleeping in a guest room in the Skull Queen's fortress. His dream began as it always did, at his hovel on the sand planet Tatooine. In the dream, he lay upon his old bed, looking up at the cracks that snaked across the ceiling.

The hovel was located in Slave Quarters Row on the edge of Mos Espa, and his old home was just as he remembered it on his last day there. It even smelled the same, with the scent of oil and grimy equipment from his workbench mingling with the dehydrated herbs and vegetables that dangled from twine in the kitchen. An inescapable haze of dust filled his room, but the blanket on his bed felt clean.

In his dream, he pushed back the blanket and brushed his fingers against the adobe wall that wrapped around his bed alcove. Feeling the wall's coolness, he wondered about the time of day. Harsh sunlight crept into his room through a narrow, louvered window and cut a shaft down through the dusty air to the intricately patterned rug spread over the dirt floor. Continuous exposure to the light had already drained most of the rug's color. Anakin decided time was not important.

The skeletal form of C-3PO teetered on his spindly legs across the room. "Good morning, Master Anakin," said the droid.

Still lying in bed, Anakin forced a smile. He felt sorry for C-3PO. He knew the droid didn't like walking around with his parts exposed.

C-3PO asked, "I trust you slept well?"

"Yes, thanks," Anakin said, then cleared his throat. Something was strange about his voice. It sounded deeper. As he rolled out of bed, he realized his legs felt heavy, and his bare feet struck the floor sooner than expected. Despite the familiar surroundings, something was different. Anakin had grown; he was no longer the boy he had been nine years ago. He was eighteen.

And he was a Jedi.

His clothes were set neatly beside his bed. He pulled on his tunic and robe, slipped his feet into his leather boots, and stood up. Facing C-3PO, he saw he was now taller than the droid. He must have looked surprised or confused because C-3PO asked, "Is everything all right, sir?"

"I think so," Anakin said. "My throat's just a bit dry." He stepped past the droid, leaving his room and entering the kitchen. On the countertop, steam rose from under the lid of a polta bean pan.

Anakin had thought he wanted a drink of water, but he realized he was searching for something else. Something he had forgotten. No, not something. Some*one*. He turned around to see C-3PO standing in his bedroom doorway, and asked, "Where's Mom?"

"Mom?" C-3PO said. He cocked his head to the side and somehow managed a quizzical expression. "Mom?" he repeated. It seemed he was unfamiliar with the word. He scratched at a wire behind his left photoreceptor, then exclaimed, "Oh, you mean your mother!"

"Yes, that's right," Anakin said. "Do you know where she is?"

"Why, I should expect she's at Watto's junkshop. I'm afraid he's had her doing quite a lot of work there, ever since you ran away."

Anakin winced. "But I didn't run away," he said. "I left. To become a Jedi."

"Oh, of course you did, sir," said C-3PO, his voice filled with good cheer. "I never meant to suggest that you abandoned any responsibilities you might have had here, when you were just a child. After all, we're so very proud of you and your achievements. Not that we actually know about what you've accomplished in the past nine years, since we've never received any messages from you, but I do get the distinct impression that your mother still cares very much about you. And she does have a vivid imagination, so she very easily assumed that you must be..."

The droid was still talking as Anakin ran out of the hovel and into the broiling radiance of Tatooine's twin suns. Although it appeared to be afternoon, when the city of Mos Espa should have been teeming with street vendors and pedestrians, there was no sign of life. Anakin felt a sense of panic. He ran as fast as he could through the empty streets until he arrived outside the tall, bell-shaped structure that was Watto's junkshop.

Like his own hovel, the junkshop appeared to be exactly as Anakin remembered it. Yet when he ducked through the shop's entrance portal and entered the cluttered interior, he found that Watto had added something new: In front of a workbench, there was a low cage with thick metal bars. A filthy figure, clothed in dirty rags, was huddled within the cage.

It was Shmi Skywalker. Anakin's mother.

She looked up at him with fear in her eyes. "Who are you?" she asked. Her voice sounded old and tired.

"It's me, Mom," Anakin said, dropping to his knees before the cage. "Anakin. Annie. I'm grown up now. I've come to rescue you."

"Anakin?" Shmi said in disbelief. She slowly shook her head. "But you can't be. You can't be here. You're gone."

"I'll get you out, Mom," Anakin said as he gripped the bars. He looked around. There was no sign of Watto.

"It *is* you," Shmi said. "It really is you."

Anakin tugged at the bars with all his might, but they would not yield. Then he remembered he was a Jedi. He could do anything! He reached to his belt, expecting to find his lightsaber, but his fingers slapped against his side. His lightsaber was gone. He tried to recall if he had clipped it to his belt before leaving his hovel, or if he had even brought it with him to Tatooine. He tried to remember when and where he had seen it last. He felt confused.

How had he arrived back on Tatooine? He could not remember.

Desperate, he glanced at Watto's tool shelf and saw a fusion-cutter and power pry-bar. He grabbed for them, but he could not pick them up. He tried again, tearing at them, but the tools would not budge. It seemed they had been welded to the shelf.

Anakin collapsed beside the cage, his head smacking against the bars. "I swear, I'll get you out!" he sobbed.

Shmi reached between the bars and pushed her oil-stained fingers through her son's blond hair. "Oh, Annie," she said. "Don't cry. Please, don't cry. I'm fine. Really, I'm fine."

"Mom, look at you! Watto left you in a cage!" Anakin said, outraged.

"No, he didn't, Annie," Shmi said sadly. "Watto didn't leave me. You did."

Suddenly, Shmi, the junkshop, and all of Tatooine were swept away from Anakin's vision, and he was engulfed in darkness. It wrapped around him like a cold, black shroud that cut him off from the entire galaxy. Unable to see, his only awareness was of the steady rise and fall of his own breathing.

Something was wrong. The breathing sounded mechanical and labored, as if it were being done through some kind of respirator. Anakin wondered if the breathing were his own, or if he had been mistaken about the sound's origin. *Perhaps*, he thought, *I'm not alone in this dark place.*

He held his breath and listened to the void. The sound of mechanized breathing stopped. And then Anakin felt his throat constricting.

The darkness coiled even tighter around him, working its way through his skin, seizing his lungs and veins and muscles and bones until he knew it was about to consume him. Then the dream ended as it always did, with Anakin trying to shout but fearing that no one, not even he, would ever hear his cry.

And then he awoke.

* * *

When Anakin's eyes opened, he found himself in his dark room in the fortress of the Skull Queen. Feeling his heart pounding, he took a deep breath and tried to relax. He wanted to clear his mind and shake off the memory of the infernal dream.

A knock at his door nearly caused him to jump. Anakin swung his legs out over the side of the bed and sat upright. "Enter."

The door slid back to reveal the trim form of Bultar Swan. Her brown eyes took in Anakin, noticing small beads of sweat on his forehead.

"A Republic Cruiser is arriving momentarily, carrying Jedi reinforcements at Obi-Wan's request," Bultar said. "Obi-Wan is waiting for us on the landing field."

"Reinforcements?" Anakin said with surprise. Rising to his feet, he asked, "Why? Another emergency?"

Bultar considered telling Anakin about the sched-

uled duel between the Skull Queen and Princess Calvaria, then decided against it. If Obi-Wan wanted to
share the details with his Padawan, it would be his
choice. She answered, "Obi-Wan called for backup
before he and I landed on Nallastia. He has a feeling
that the Fondor system remains threatened."

"A *feeling*?" Anakin said in disbelief. "He called
for backup without any hard evidence?"

In a severe tone, Bultar answered, "If you question
your Master's methods, you might confront him
directly."

"Please forgive me," Anakin said hastily. "I meant
no disrespect. I spoke without thinking." Catching
his disheveled reflection in a mirror that hung above
a wooden trunk, he reached up and used his sleeve
to wipe away the sweat from his forehead. Aware that
Bultar was looking at him, he said, "If I may
ask...when you sleep, do you ever have visions of
your homeworld or family?"

Bultar shook her head. "I was raised at the Jedi
Temple. My home has always been with the Jedi."

"Then can you tell me, what *do* you dream?"

Choosing her words carefully, Bultar said, "I am
not your Master, and I am not certain that my answer
would help. If you are having difficulty sleeping, you
should talk with Obi-Wan."

"I already have," Anakin said. "And I have followed
his instructions to meditate before sleeping. Yet, I
sometimes have disturbing visions. I only ask for
your insight because I do not wish to fail Obi-Wan."

Bultar remained silent.

"Please," Anakin said.

Bultar sighed. "When I sleep, as when I meditate, I usually visualize wide-open spaces and fields of color."

Anakin's eyebrows lifted slightly. "You said 'usually.' Does darkness ever intrude?"

Bultar nodded. "Sometimes I see what appear to be dark clouds, but they never last for long. I can control them. I imagine winds to drive back the clouds, or to transform them into gentle rains. I find such thoughts to have a calming effect."

"I see," Anakin said. "Can you also control your nightmares?"

Bultar's eyes narrowed. Anakin sensed she was studying him the way she might study an especially difficult puzzle or perhaps a dangerous creature. Then calmly, as if to a child, she replied, "Jedi don't have nightmares."

Anakin appeared to consider this, then said, "Of course."

"I'll wait in the hall while you get cleaned up," Bultar said. She turned away, and the door slid shut, leaving Anakin alone in the dark room.

Anakin looked again to the mirror and stared hard at his reflection. He grimaced. "Jedi don't have nightmares," he muttered to himself.

"Jedi...don't...have...nightmares."

He wished it were true.

CHAPTER THREE

Outside the Skull Queen's fortress, Anakin and Bultar walked toward Obi-Wan, who stood at the edge of the landing field near a row of Nallastian shuttles. Obi-Wan's neck was tilted back as he looked up into the night sky. Anakin and Bultar followed his gaze to see a descending Republic Cruiser. As the ship touched down on the field, Obi-Wan glanced at Anakin and asked, "I hope you enjoyed your short rest, Padawan."

"Yes, Master," Anakin replied. But as soon as the words were out of his mouth, he thought of his conversation with Bultar. Hoping to convince Bultar that he was not concealing anything from Obi-Wan, Anakin quickly added, "I mean, not entirely, Master. I experienced dark visions."

Obi-Wan turned to Anakin. "You also sense more danger for the Fondor system?"

"Possibly," Anakin said, although he suspected a negative response would have been more accurate. His nightmare had had nothing to do with Fondor or Nallastia.

The cruiser's hatch opened and a landing ramp extended to the field. Seconds later, two robed figures appeared on the ramp. The first was Jedi Master Kit Fisto, an amphibious Nautolan from Glee Anselm. The second was Jedi Master Mace Windu.

Anakin was surprised to see Mace Windu. As a senior member of the Jedi High Council, Master Windu usually directed missions from the Jedi Temple on Coruscant, so Anakin regarded his presence on Nallastia as most unexpected. If Obi-Wan and Bultar were surprised, they did not show it.

Obi-Wan bowed and said, "Greetings, Masters Windu and Fisto."

"Greetings," Mace Windu said.

Kit Fisto said, "We were attending the dedication of a memorial to Yarael Poof on Quermia when we intercepted your request for reinforcements."

Obi-Wan nodded, his expression grim. Yarael Poof, a Quermian, had been a member of the Jedi Council until his untimely death, four years earlier. His absence remained deeply felt among all Jedi.

Mace Windu asked, "Why did you summon us, Obi-Wan?"

Obi-Wan informed Mace Windu and Kit Fisto of recent events, from the emergence of the replica *Sun Runner*, to the recovery of the Lost Stars of Nallastia and subsequent rescue of the two zoologists. When Obi-Wan had finished, Mace Windu said, "You were wise to call for backup when you did. As Kit Fisto and I arrived in the Fondor system, we also sensed danger."

Bultar Swan cleared her throat and looked at Obi-Wan. Obi-Wan scowled.

"There is something you have not told us?" Mace Windu asked.

"Princess Calvaria has challenged the Skull Queen to a duel," Obi-Wan said. "It seems they intend to fight for my hand in marriage."

Anakin raised his eyebrows. "*What*?"

"The challenge was made while you were resting," Obi-Wan explained. "Obviously, I did nothing to encourage the queen or princess. I regret I have been so far unable to persuade them to call off the duel."

Anakin asked, "If you *were* to marry, would that make you the Skull King?"

Obi-Wan shot a stern look at his Padawan. "I'm not getting married, Anakin."

"Of course not, Master," Anakin said.

"When is the duel scheduled?" Mace Windu asked.

"In less than an hour," Obi-Wan said

"Bring me to the Skull Queen," Mace Windu said. "I will resolve this matter at once."

Moments after the Jedi entered the Skull Queen's fortress, a Nallastian shuttle lifted up from the landing field, then blasted off in the direction of Fondor. Seated behind the controls, the shuttle's single passenger breathed a sigh of relief. It had not been easy to leave the fortress and landing field unnoticed, but it had been necessary.

After all, Princess Calvaria could not think of any other way to escape her problems and be with her true love.

* * *

Fondor Spaceport was a two-kilometer-long tubular orbital station, lined with 160 pressurized hangar bays. In one of the larger public-access hangars, Senator Rodd watched the docking port and waited for the arrival of Groodo the Hutt. To avoid detection by Space Patrol authorities, Rodd wore a heavy, hooded robe that covered his uniform and almost completely concealed his face. As an extra precaution, he had sprayed the robe with a foul-smelling chemical that encouraged people to keep their distance. Unfortunately, Rodd had very sensitive nostrils and could hardly wait to get out of the stinking robe. He was considering changing into a different disguise when Groodo's starship came into view through the docking port, then entered the hangar.

Groodo had spared few luxuries on his private cruiser, but like most Hutts, his taste was questionable. The cruiser had broad fins, large oval viewports, and a lurid color scheme of red, orange, and yellow; everything was designed for maximum visibility and to show off Groodo's considerable wealth. Despite the fact that Senator Rodd had been anxiously awaiting Groodo's cruiser, the actual sight of it made him shudder.

The cruiser's hatch opened, and a Hutt slithered down the landing ramp. Looking at the hooded humanoid figure, the Hutt said, "Senator Rodd?"

"Hush!" said Rodd. "I'm in disguise."

"Oh," said the Hutt. "Sorry, um…mister. My dad's waiting for you on board."

Confused, Rodd asked, "Your dad?"

"Yeah, you know…" In a loud whisper, the Hutt said, "Groodo."

"Ah," Rodd said, realizing that the Hutt before him was Groodo's son, Boonda. Rodd followed Boonda up the ramp and into the cruiser. When the hatch shut behind them, Boonda's wide, slitted nostrils flared.

"Gee, Senator," Boonda said, sniffing the air. "What's that crazy scent you're wearing?"

"A synthetic aroma designed to keep people away."

"Really?" Boonda grinned. "I kind of like it."

Boonda led Rodd into a plush cabin lined with striped animal pelts. There, they found Groodo lounging on an arrangement of wide pillows and a human female sitting in a molded-plastoid chair. Wearing a drab, gray uniform, the woman had short dark hair and extremely pale skin. Rodd did not recognize her, but looking at her complexion, he concluded that she rarely exposed herself to sunlight.

"Hullo, Senator," Groodo said. Gesturing to the seated woman, he added, "Allow me to introduce you to Hurlo Holowan. She engineered the droids that piloted the fake *Sun Runner*. Don't worry, you can talk freely. She knows better than to squeal on us."

Rodd nodded at Holowan and said, "How do you do?"

Wincing at the smell of Rodd's robe, Holowan said, "I've wondered what kind of man would be willing to sell out his own world for Groodo's credits."

Rodd shrugged. "I like money. And I'm not so fond of people."

"Then we should get along fine," Holowan said coolly. "What happened to the droids on the *Sun Runner* replica?"

"They were destroyed by Jedi, along with the entire ship," Rodd answered.

"What a waste," Holowan said. "I put a lot of time into them."

"Let's get down to business." Groodo chuckled, slapping his meaty hands together. "Senator, I promised you a fortune in return for your help in putting Fondor out of the starship- manufacturing business. Now, I followed your instructions to the letter, constructing the fake *Sun Runner* to distract your people as well as the Nallastians, supplying the weapons to wipe out Fondor's starship yards, and so on. You were supposed to prevent any Jedi from meddling. What went wrong?"

"The Jedi were more cunning than I realized," Rodd admitted. "However, they are presently on Fondor's moon, Nallastia. If we are to fulfill our plan to bring Fondor to ruin, we must act now. Did you bring more droids?"

Groodo nodded. "Twelve. Various models. In the cargo bay."

Holowan added, "No one will be able to trace the droids back to us. I've pre-programmed them to think they are soldiers of the Droid Control Army, something I made up."

Groodo chuckled. "Tracing the droids to us would

require evidence. By the time we're done with the spaceport, there won't be any evidence left."

"But only twelve droids?" Rodd asked, surprised by the modest number. "Will that be enough to destroy the entire spaceport?"

"Twelve is plenty," Holowan said. "After we set them up and fly out of here, I'll operate them by remote."

"I see," Rodd said. "And how long will it take them to seize control of the spaceport?"

"It depends," Holowan said. "Do you have the spaceport's security codes?"

"Of course."

Holowan smiled. "Then it won't take long at all."

Minutes later, the droids were ready, and Groodo's starship made a hasty exit from the spaceport.

* * *

Under any other traveling conditions, Princess Calvaria would have noticed the incredibly bright-colored starship with enormous, decorative fins that sped away from the Fondor Spaceport. But as her shuttle approached a large hangar on the spaceport's planet-facing side, Calvaria was not looking at other starships. Her mind was on something else. More specifically, her mind was on *someone* else, and he was waiting for her in the hangar.

He was a young, dark-haired man who wore grease-stained mechanic's coveralls. The man watched anxiously as the Nallastian shuttle glided through the hangar's docking port and landed on a platform. The shuttle's hatch opened, and Calvaria stepped out onto the platform. The man ran to her, and they embraced.

"I was afraid you would not meet me," the man said.

"I promised I would, Rench," Calvaria replied.

The man pushed his fingers through Calvaria's hair and declared, "I love you so much, Klara."

Calvaria closed her eyes and held Rench tight. Growing up as Princess of the Skull Clan, she had always wondered how people might regard her if they did not know she was royalty. She had been on a trade mission to Fondor when she met Rench and introduced herself as Klara, an aide to Margravine Quenelle, which wasn't so very far from the truth. She had not expected to fall in love with Rench and felt awful for having lied to him about her true identity.

"Rench," she said. "There is something I must tell you."

"Yes, Klara?"

Before Calvaria could say more, a loud, electric crackle filled the air. The sound came from a comm speaker that was set above a door that led out of the hangar and into a station corridor. Suddenly, the hangar's main lights went out. As several emergency glow rods switched on, an inhuman voice droned from the comm speaker: "Attention! Fondor

Spaceport is now under the control of the Droid Control Army. All organics will surrender at once. Anyone who attempts to leave the station will be vaporized."

Calvaria squeezed Rench's hand. He said, "Droid Control Army? I've never heard of them, but it sure doesn't sound good."

"There's a long-range comm in my shuttle!" Calvaria exclaimed. "We'll try to call for help!"

CHAPTER FOUR

"I *do* appreciate your concern, Master Windu, but I cannot call off the duel with my daughter," the Skull Queen said. "Our customs dictate that only the instigator can withdraw the challenge. Unless Calvaria does so, I am bound by Nallastian tradition to fight her."

Mace Windu maintained a calm expression as he faced the Skull Queen. They were in the Skull Queen's dressing room in her fortress, where a team of servants were fitting their leader with armor made from animal bones. They stood before a wall that was decorated with a broad tapestry of the Skull Queen and her late husband, a bearded man with green eyes. Obi-Wan, Anakin, and Bultar stood behind Master Windu and listened attentively.

Mace Windu replied, "I regret you do not understand, Your Highness. I am no longer *urging* you and your daughter to reconsider the duel. I am *telling* you there will not be a duel."

The Skull Queen was taken aback. "You're saying you won't allow it?"

"Yes," Mace Windu stated. "A Jedi is a living being, not a prize to be won."

The Skull Queen looked to Obi-Wan and said, "Do you not believe you are worth fighting for?"

"I have dedicated my life to helping those in need," Obi-Wan said. "If you and Princess Calvaria have one need, it is to learn to communicate without fighting. If you continue with the duel, you will only be hurting each other and doing me a great disservice."

The Skull Queen thought about this, then turned to one of her servants and said, "Go to Calvaria's chambers and bring her here at once." As the servant left the room, the Skull Queen stepped away from her other servants to admire her reflection in a tall mirror. "It has been nearly seven years since I last wore this armor," she said as she placed a horned-skull helmet onto her head. "It's nice to know it still fits." Turning to face Obi-Wan, she removed the helmet and handed it to the nearest servant.

Obi-Wan asked, "This means you will not fight Calvaria?"

The Skull Queen nodded. "I never meant to insult you, Obi-Wan. And I never intended to harm Calvaria. I only wanted..." Her lip trembled, then she turned away to face the tapestry on her wall. "I only wanted to be happy...again."

Obi-Wan felt his throat go dry. He was aware that Anakin, Bultar, and the Skull Queen's servants were looking at him, wondering how or if he would respond. Before he could utter a word, Mace Windu said, "Honesty takes courage, Your Highness. And healing takes time."

Just then, the servant who had been sent to get Calvaria returned to the Skull Queen's dressing

38

room. "Your Highness!" the servant said. "The princess is gone! She left this."

The servant handed a small, disk-shaped hologram projector to the Skull Queen, who activated the device. A flickering three-dimensional image of Calvaria materialized from the projector, and her recorded voice spoke. "Dearest Mother. I have no interest in the Jedi, nor any intention of dueling with you. I said those things to distract you so I could escape the marriage to Prince Alto. I am in love with a mechanic from Fondor and have gone to be with him. By the time you hear this message, I will be leaving for another star system. I wish we could have resolved our differences. Please do not hate me. I love you, Mother." The hologram flicked off.

"Why, the cunning, lovesick firemanx!" the Skull Queen said. "If she doesn't marry Prince Alto, it will insult the Raptor Clan. They will declare war on us!"

"An insult hardly justifies a war," Mace Windu said.

The Skull Queen laughed. "Try telling that to the Raptor Clan."

A Nallastian guard entered the Skull Queen's room and said, "Excuse me, Your Highness, but one of our shuttles has been stolen from the landing field."

"Calvaria took it," the Skull Queen said. "Was the shuttle equipped with a tracker?"

"Yes. Its signal is coming from a hangar at Fondor Spaceport."

"Maybe I can catch her there," said the Skull Queen. She crossed the room to a cabinet that opened to reveal a private comm console. The Jedi watched as the Skull Queen entered a code into the comm. After waiting several seconds, she said, "That's strange. There's no response from the Spaceport. I'll try a different frequency."

The Skull Queen adjusted the controls on her console. "—anyone hear me?!" a young woman's voice squawked from the comm. "Can anyone out there hear me?"

The Skull Queen recognized the voice immediately. "Calvaria?"

"Mother! I'm on Fondor Spaceport! Droids have taken over the entire facility! They're rounding up all life-forms and—"

The transmission was cut off by a loud burst of static, then another voice—not human—stated, "Fondor Spaceport is under the control of the Droid Control Army. All docking ports are shielded. Do not attempt to land. Fondor's senator will receive our demands in one hour." Then the message was repeated.

Obi-Wan looked to Anakin and said, "More droids. Perhaps like those that were on the fake *Sun Runner*."

"Perhaps this so-called army is picking up where the other droids left off," Anakin suggested. "They might intend to use the spaceport as a weapon."

"*What*?" gasped the Skull Queen.

Obi-Wan did not want to alarm the Skull Queen but admitted, "Anakin may be right."

Kit Fisto said, "For all we know, this may be a trap, designed to lure us away from Nallastia."

"Then stay here if you must," said the Skull Queen as she retrieved her helmet. "I'm going to rescue Calvaria. Is anyone with me?"

Obi-Wan, Anakin, Bultar, and Kit Fisto turned to face Mace Windu. The senior Jedi said, "The droids' message states they will issue demands in one hour. If that's true, then they must be confident that no one will attempt a rescue mission *before* they issue their demands. If it's not true, then they may be using the next hour to prepare for even greater chaos. The droids must be stopped now." He looked at Obi-Wan. "However, Kit Fisto may be right about a trap. Some of us should remain here."

Obi-Wan asked, "What happens if Prince Alto and his Raptor Clan come looking for Calvaria?"

"We will deal with the Raptor Clan *after* we find the princess," Mace Windu replied. After quickly deciding which Jedi would remain on Nallastia, Mace Windu turned to the others and said, "Let us not waste any more time."

At this point, you must decide whether to continue reading this adventure, or to play your own adventure in the Star Wars Adventures *The Hostage Princess* Game Book.

To play your own adventure, turn to the first page of the Game Book and follow the directions you find there.

To continue reading this adventure, turn the page!

CHAPTER FIVE

Standing in the Skull Queen's fortress, Obi-Wan and Anakin watched Mace Windu, Bultar Swan, and Kit Fisto leave with the Skull Queen. Obi-Wan turned to Anakin and was not surprised to see the young man's sullen expression.

"Why did Master Windu decide that *we* should remain on Nallastia?" Anakin asked. "Is it because he thinks I am not ready for such a mission?"

"Master Windu's orders are not for us to ponder, but to respect," Obi-Wan replied. "And speaking of respect, it seems to me that Master Windu has given us a great deal of his."

Anakin shook his head. "Forgive me, Master, but I do not understand. Master Windu selected Bultar Swan and Kit Fisto to join him on the mission to Fondor Spaceport, leaving us behind?"

"We were *not* left behind, Padawan," Obi-Wan said. "By assigning us to remain here, Master Windu left us with the responsibility to protect and defend all of Nallastia from hostile intruders. When one thinks about it, that's quite a lot to entrust to anyone."

"I didn't think of it that way," Anakin admitted, still wishing he were on his way to Fondor Spaceport. "You really think Master Windu trusts me?"

"If he didn't, I suspect you and I would be forever stuck on Coruscant."

"I guess you're right," Anakin said with a smile.

Obi-Wan smiled back, hoping that Anakin would be satisfied with this explanation. In truth, Obi-Wan suspected that Mace Windu had assigned him and Anakin to stay on Nallastia for reasons that had nothing to do with Anakin's relatively limited experience in combat. Granted, it was just a hunch, but Obi-Wan had a feeling that Mace Windu was trying to do him a favor by keeping him away from the Skull Queen and her unwanted romantic attentions.

Does she truly believe she loves me? As soon as the thought struck Obi-Wan, it began to gnaw at him. And much to his surprise, he was not entirely relieved to be out of the Skull Queen's presence. He knew she could handle herself in a fight, but he was surprised to suddenly feel very concerned for her safety.

He wished she had remained on Nallastia.

* * *

Mace Windu exited the fortress with the Skull Queen, Bultar Swan, and Kit Fisto. Although it was night, Mace could see quite clearly. Overhead, in the star-filled sky, the planet Fondor appeared in a gibbous phase and reflected sunlight down upon Nallastia's surface. Mace and the others were headed for the landing field, where rested the red-painted Republic Cruiser, when the Skull Queen exclaimed, "Wait!"

"What is it?" Mace asked.

"Your Republic Cruiser is an unarmed diplomatic ship," the Skull Queen said. "Since Fondor Spaceport is protected by deflector shields, it would be wise to travel with the power gems—the Stars of Nallastia."

Mace looked to Bultar Swan, who said, "She has a point. The cruiser doesn't have weapons, and the gems *are* able to knock out force fields."

"Where are the power gems now?" Mace asked.

"Atop the Trinity Stones," the Skull Queen replied.

"Take me there," Mace Windu said. Turning to Bultar and Kit, he said, "Go to the cruiser and tell the captain to prepare for liftoff."

Kit and Bultar ran for the ship. The Skull Queen motioned to Mace and said, "This way."

Following the Skull Queen, Mace rounded the fortress's outer wall to see three tall megaliths. Armed Nallastian warriors stood guard, defending the sacred power gems that rested atop the Trinity Stones. The Skull Queen ordered the warriors to retrieve the power gems from the megaliths, but Mace raised his hands and said, "Allow me."

The warriors and Skull Queen watched with amazement as the three power gems rose from the megaliths and quickly traveled through the air toward Mace. The moment the power gems lost contact with the megaliths, a force field activated between the Trinity Stones. As Mace caught the blue and red gems with his left hand and the green gem with his right, the Skull Queen faced her warriors and commanded, "Do not allow anyone near the Trinity Stones until I return with the power gems." The warriors bowed, and the Skull Queen ran after Mace, who was already heading back to the landing field.

As Mace walked, he removed an expandable pouch from his utility belt and placed the power gems inside them. He was walking past a tree at the edge of the landing field, when he noticed what appeared to be two long, dark logs lying in his path. But as he drew closer, the two forms moved, and Mace realized they were not logs at all. They were six-legged Nallastian lizards with powerful jaws and sharp teeth. Apparently seeing him as a threat, the two reptiles hissed and prepared to attack.

Without breaking his stride, Mace glared at the reptiles and said, "Move." Something in the man's voice struck the reptiles with raw terror. Yelping, the reptiles skittered out of Mace's way and off the landing field.

"Your powers are impressive," the Skull Queen said as she caught up with Mace.

"A Jedi's powers are meant to serve the Force, not impress," Mace responded.

"Think what you like," the Skull Queen said, matching Mace's gait. "But I suspect most non-Jedi are fascinated by your abilities."

"Some are fascinated, others aren't," Mace commented as they neared the Republic Cruiser. He added, "Most are envious and want the powers for themselves."

The Skull Queen laughed. "You suspect I am interested in Obi-Wan because of his powers?"

"What I suspect of your interests is not important," Mace answered as he led the Skull Queen up the cruiser's landing ramp. "What I know for a fact is that Obi-Wan is a Jedi and will always be a Jedi. It is his destiny."

The Skull Queen chose not to comment.

Inside the Republic Cruiser's entrance forum, Mace Windu and the Skull Queen were greeted by the ship's captain, Nico Medina. Captain Medina said, "Bultar Swan and Kit Fisto are already seated in the salon pod."

"We'll accompany you to the bridge," Mace said. Opening the pouch that contained the Stars of Nallastia, Mace added, "According to the Nallastians, these gems should allow us to pass though the spaceport's defensive shields."

"They *will* work," the Skull Queen insisted.

"Of course," said Captain Medina. *Gems that could disable a force field?* He'd heard of stranger things.

They entered a lift that delivered them to a corridor that led to the bridge. As they walked to the bridge, Mace told Medina, "Instruct the pilots to fly directly to Fondor Spaceport."

"Yes, Master Windu."

Mace and the Skull Queen eased into two seats in the small lounge behind the cockpit. They were still strapping themselves into their seat's safety harnesses when the ship lifted off from the landing field.

Seconds later, the ship suddenly lurched hard to one side, and excited shouts came from the cockpit. Glancing through the doorway that separated the lounge from the captain and two co-pilots, Mace saw the problem: The crew was under attack by a large purple snake.

"It's a venrap!" the Skull Queen said. "It must have slithered on board while the ship was on the landing field!"

The venrap was already coiled tightly around the seated captain and two co-pilots, and appeared to be squeezing the life from them. Out of control, the Republic Cruiser's nose dropped, sending the ship into a steep dive.

Mace unfastened his safety harness and sprang from the lounge. Tumbling toward the cockpit, he slammed into the back of the captain's seat. The giant snake uncoiled itself from the captain and co-pilots, and as the three humans slumped forward in their seats, Mace realized they had been rendered unconscious. The venrap turned its purple head to face Mace, hissed, then opened its sharp-fanged maw.

Mace was reluctant to take any life, but he knew there was no other option. He had to regain control of the ship immediately. In a swift, fluid movement, Mace drew his lightsaber, activated its blade, and was about to behead the snake when a vibroblade sailed past his side and struck the snake between the eyes, killing it instantly. With the vibroblade embedded in its skull, the snake's lifeless body flopped to the cockpit floor.

Mace glanced back to the lounge, where the Skull Queen was still poised with one arm extended. *Nice throw*, Mace thought as he turned to the cockpit's viewport. It appeared the cruiser was only seconds away from crashing into the Nallastian jungle.

Stepping past the unconscious co-pilots, Mace grabbed the controls and pulled back hard. The cruiser responded instantly, arcing up and away from Nallastia's surface. The snake's dead body slid back down the corridor and into the lounge.

From the cockpit's comm came the voice of Bultar Swan, who demanded, "What's going on up there?"

"We had a little situation," Mace answered. "Are you and Kit all right?"

Bultar replied, "Yes, Master Windu."

After the cruiser left Nallastia's atmosphere and entered space, Mace entered a series of coordinates into the navi-computer, then checked on the captain and co-pilots. The crew was in stable condition, and Captain Medina was already starting to wake up.

Mace turned back to the Skull Queen, who was prying her vibroblade from the venrap's skull. Mace said, "The cruiser's autopilot will take us to Fondor Spaceport. We'll be there in a few minutes."

"I hope there will be no more delays," the Skull Queen said as she returned the vibroblade to a sheath at her side. "I am anxious to see my daughter."

CHAPTER SIX

Streaking across space, the Republic Cruiser soon arrived within sight of Fondor Spaceport. Mace Windu and the Skull Queen were seated in the co-pilot seats, having moved the co-pilots to the lounge.

As the cruiser neared the spaceport, the comm system intercepted an automated audio transmission: "Do not attempt to land," said a non-human voice. "Fondor Spaceport is under the control of the Droid Control Army. All docking ports are shielded. Do not attempt to land." The message repeated itself. Mace Windu switched off the comm.

According to the Republic Cruiser's sensor array, all of Fondor Spaceport was protected by strong deflector shields, invisible force fields that had been adjusted to prevent any starship from entering the hangars. From what Mace could see through the cruiser's viewport, the spaceport had two deflector-shield projectors—geodesic domes that hugged the station's hull-like massive blisters.

Mace reached for the pouch that contained the power gems. Opening the pouch, he asked, "How exactly do these gems work? Do we have to place them on top of the deflector-shield projectors?"

"That method is reserved for Trinity Stones," the Skull Queen replied. "According to legend, all we have to do is bring the gems within range of the force field. The gems project an aura. They do not have to leave your cruiser."

Mace steered the cruiser closer to the massive spaceport. When he had closed the distance to fifty meters, the spaceport's exterior was suddenly illuminated by a brilliant flash of blue light.

"The deflector shields are down!" Mace said.

"Now *you* sound impressed," the Skull Queen noted.

Mace adjusted a sensor to home in on the signal from the tracker on Princess Calvaria's shuttle. Following the signal, Mace steered the cruiser into the hangar that contained the Nallastian shuttle and landed beside it.

Mace and the Skull Queen left the cockpit and rode the lift to the cruiser's entrance forum, where they were reunited with Kit Fisto and Bultar Swan. Stepping out of the Republic Cruiser and onto the hangar's landing pad, the group saw that Princess Calvaria's shuttle looked undamaged. In fact, the hangar's entire interior appeared normal, except for the fact that there weren't any living beings in sight.

The Skull Queen and Mace inspected Calvaria's shuttle and found no one on board. Exiting the shuttle, they looked for clues that might have suggested the direction Calvaria took when she left the hangar. Near a stack of empty cargo containers, Mace noticed a single sheet of plastoid plating lying on the floor. Wondering how the plastoid plate came to rest in that location, he picked it up and examined it.

Then he heard a noise: *Gonk-gonk-gonk*. The sound came from a box-shaped, two-legged GNK power droid, which wobbled out from behind one of the cargo containers. Power droids were ambulatory fusion generators, a common sight in starship hangars and docking yards. Mace noticed there were more plastoid sheets on top of one cargo container, and he imagined that the droid may have accidentally knocked over the one that he had found on the floor.

Suddenly, the power droid's upper casing flipped open, revealing a rapid-repeating blaster. The lethally modified droid fired off a burst of laser bolts. Kit, Bultar, and the Skull Queen dove for cover.

But not Mace. With one hand, he held the plastoid sheet like a shield in front of his body, as he drew his lightsaber with his other hand. As laser bolts hammered at the plastoid sheet, Mace advanced to the power droid and lashed out with his blazing blade, neatly severing the blaster from the droid's frame.

The power droid lurched forward, trying to stomp on Mace's foot, but Mace landed a powerful kick on the droid's side. The droid fell back into an empty cargo container, and Mace moved quickly to seal the container, trapping the droid.

As the cargo droid thumped and bumped within the container, Kit said, "Can we assume that we've had our first encounter with the Droid Control Army?"

Mace answered, "We should assume nothing until we learn who programmed the droids, and why. Right now, I'm more concerned about finding Princess Calvaria and the other beings on the spaceport."

"Fondor Spaceport is quite large," said the Skull

Queen. "We'll have a better chance of finding the captives if we split up."

Kit and Bultar looked to Mace, waiting for his decision. Mace said, "Agreed. Move out."

Four doorways provided exits from the hangar, so Bultar, Kit, and the Skull Queen each left through a different doorway. Mace was heading for the remaining doorway when he saw an open vent set in the wall above a bulkhead. Listening carefully, Mace heard the faint sound of mechanical beeps and whistles.

More droids.

Mace climbed up the bulkhead and slipped into the open vent. He crawled along through the vent until he arrived at a room filled with computers. It was a spaceport security office, and there were two cylindrical-bodied, dome-headed astromech droids on either side of the chamber. One astromech was jacked into the spaceport's main computer, and the other monitored a technical readout on a sensor screen.

Mace lowered himself down from the vent, and the two droids rotated their domes to look at him through their photoreceptors. The droids appeared harmless, but then each flipped open more concealed panels to extend a manipulator-gripped fusion-cutter, a cutting tool that emitted a high-energy plasma beam.

With incredible speed, Mace drew his humming lightsaber and leaped between the two astromechs. One droid turned quickly as it fired its fusion-cutter, accidentally shooting the other droid, destroying it instantly. Mace brought his lightsaber down through the shooter, and the astromech screeched as it was cut in half. Both droids fell in pieces to the floor.

Mace deactivated his lightsaber. Returning the weapon to his belt, he stepped past the smoldering remains of the two astromechs and moved to the security office's computer terminal. He then examined the displays on several screens. Except for the spaceport's disabled deflector-shield projectors, all systems appeared to be operational. Mace hoped the spaceport's computer would reveal the number of enemy droids on board, and also the location of any captured life-forms.

He tinkered with the controls until he found the information he wanted. According to the spaceport's security records, Fondor Spaceport had been infiltrated and seized by a total of twelve unauthorized droids, who had then forced all life-forms into Hangar 173. At present, six droids were guarding the captives. Mace had already defeated three enemy droids, which left—in addition to the six in Hangar 173—three more droids at large elsewhere in the spaceport. Unfortunately, the security computer was unable to determine the location of the three unaccounted for droids.

Mace located a lift tube at the other end of the security office. Entering the lift, he found a voice-activated control panel on the lift's wall. He said,

"Hangar 173." Instantly, the lift sped through the tube. Less than ten seconds later, the lift slowed to a stop and the door slid open. Mace stepped out.

The lift had delivered him to the end of a catwalk that extended across Hangar 173. Peering over the edge of the catwalk, Mace looked down at the hangar floor. Just as he had seen on the video display in the security office, six droids stood guard around their large group of captives on the hangar's landing pad.

The six droids were all FX medical assistants, each equipped with twenty precise manipulator arms and a single primary grasping arm. Like the power droid and two astromechs that Mace had already encountered, the medical droids would not have appeared out of place on a space station under normal circumstances, which was probably how they had been able to infiltrate Fondor Spaceport so easily. However, the circumstances were hardly normal, and instead of wielding medical tools, each FX unit brandished numerous deadly weapons. Also, all six droids were mounted on treadwell bases, allowing them greater mobility than any standard-issue FX unit.

So far, none of the medical droids had noticed Mace's presence on the catwalk. As he considered his next move, he realized he was within reach of the hangar's tractor-beam projector, a device that produced a powerful, maneuverable force field that could capture and move objects. Normally, the tractor-beam projector was used to safely move starships through the hangar's docking port, but since three of the six droids were positioned near the docking port, Mace had another use in mind for the projector.

With great stealth, he moved behind the controls of the hangar's tractor-beam projector. Aiming for the three droids that were close to the docking port, he activated the beam and trapped them in its force field. Before the other three FX units realized what was happening, Mace pushed a lever, sent the trapped three through the docking port and into space, then switched off the projector. Outside the spaceport, the three ejected droids tumbled off in the direction of Fondor's sun.

Below Mace, on the hangar's landing pad, the three remaining FX medical droids rotated their disk-shaped heads to look up, then raised their weapons to his position on the catwalk. Because of the droids' proximity to their captives, Mace could not risk using the hangar's tractor-beam projector again. He knew he had to draw the droids' fire away from the beings on the landing pad.

"Get down!" he shouted to the droids' captives. As dozens of humans and aliens dropped and hugged the landing pad, the three medical droids fired their weapons at the Jedi on the catwalk.

Mace ducked behind the tractor-beam projector, while laser bolts pinged and popped all around him. Then he realized the droids were moving around on the floor to get a clear shot at him. Bolting from the projector, he sped across the catwalk until he reached a service gantry. As a spray of laser bolts hammered at the gantry, Mace spied an electromagnetic pincer crane suspended from the hangar's ceiling, directly above one of the three remaining FX units.

Drawing and activating his lightsaber, Mace leaped out from the gantry and dragged his lightsaber through the pincer crane's ceiling mount. The Jedi Master landed on the hangar floor at the same instant that the crane crashed down on the FX unit, crushing the droid.

Exposed on the hangar floor, Mace watched the last two FX units roll forward on their treadwell mounts, moving into attack position. The droid on his right sought defensive cover behind a tall column, but the droid on his left was less careful, and moved past the edge of a deep, rectangular hydrolift well. The well was typically used to transport cargo to a lower level of the spaceport, but as with the tractor-beam projector, Mace thought of a different use for the hangar's utilities.

Reaching out with the Force, Mace pushed at the droid to his left, sending it over the edge of the hydrolift well. The FX unit fell down the shaft, and its impact produced a satisfying explosion.

The last FX unit was about to fire at Mace from behind the nearby column when, without warning, one of the captives sprang from the landing pad and raced at the droid. It appeared that the captive, a young man in mechanic's coveralls, was making a brave effort to stop the droid from harming the Jedi. But before the man could reach the droid, the FX unit spun and struck him with a stun baton. Instantly paralyzed, the man collapsed to the hangar floor.

"Rench!" shouted a young woman from the landing pad. Rising from the cowering crowd, the woman ran toward the fallen man. Mace recognized the woman immediately. He had seen her holographic image at the Skull Queen's fortress.

The woman was Princess Calvaria.

CHAPTER SEVEN

"This doesn't look good," Groodo the Hutt grumbled.

"There's only one droid left in the hangar?" Senator Rodd shouted in panic.

"Shut up and let me concentrate!" Hurlo Holowan shouted back as she manipulated the remote control for the last FX unit.

Groodo, Rodd, and Holowan were on Groodo's cruiser, and Rodd was peering over Holowan's shoulder to look at the viewscreen that was set before her. It displayed the view of the last heavily modified FX medical assistant droid, one of six that Holowan had unleashed upon Fondor Spaceport. The six FX units had performed well, rounding up all the life-forms on the spaceport and bringing them to Hangar 173. But then the Jedi had knocked out the spaceport's shields and busted into the hangar. That hadn't been expected. Now there was indeed only one FX unit left.

Groodo considered ordering Holowan to destroy the spaceport immediately. The plan had been so simple—seize control of the spaceport, wait until its orbit carried it over the planet Fondor's most important surface factories, then send the entire spaceport crashing down upon the factories. There was never any intention for Holowan's droids to issue demands; Groodo simply needed one hour to allow the spaceport to reach the right point in Fondor's orbit. The spaceport wasn't in position yet, but Groodo didn't want any more trouble with the Jedi. He clutched at

his thick-skinned chest, took a deep breath, and prepared to give the order for an early destruction.

"Wait!" Rodd exclaimed. "Look there!" He jabbed
a finger at the viewscreen, where the image of a
woman was running toward a man who lay on the
floor near the last FX unit. "That woman! She's
Princess Calvaria of Nallastia! We have to get her off
the spaceport before it drops!"

"You must be kidding," Holowan said.

"She's the daughter of the Skull Queen!" Rodd
explained. "She's worth infinitely more alive than
dead!" He turned to Groodo and said, "Think of the
ransom!"

Groodo gave his order. "Grab the princess,
Holowan."

Mace Windu wished Princess Calvaria had not run
to the fallen man. She was so close to the last
weapon-wielding FX unit that Mace dared not attack.
As Calvaria neared the man she called Rench, the FX
unit reached out with three of its manipulator arms
and snared her. Calvaria struggled, but the droid
used the stun baton on her, and the princess went
limp. Lifting her unconscious form, the droid used
four other manipulator arms to aim one blaster pistol
at the princess, a second in the direction of the captives on the landing pad, a third at Rench's motionless
form, and a fourth pistol at Mace.

The FX unit stared at Mace through a black
photoreceptor, as if challenging the Jedi Master to

make a move. Mace knew the droid would not hesi-tate to pull any one of the blasters' triggers.

Suddenly, Bultar Swan entered the hangar via the lift tube, and Kit Fisto ran in through a doorway from an adjoining hangar. The two Jedi had their lightsabers drawn.

Keeping his voice calm, Mace told his allies, "Lower your weapons."

Bultar and Kit deactivated their blades. Still carrying the princess, the droid slowly backed away toward a doorway, through which it exited the hangar.

Facing the other Jedi, Mace said, "Stay here and protect these beings. I'm going after that droid."

Mace left the hangar through the same doorway that the FX unit had used and entered a corridor lined with ten closed doorways. He looked at the corridor floor, but the droid had not left any tracks.

Closing his eyes, Mace cautiously moved forward and listened for movement beyond the doors. Hearing a faint clattering sound from behind one door, he drew his weapon and put his hand to the door. It was locked. Mace drove his lightsaber through the area of the door's locking mechanism, then retracted his weapon and kicked the door.

He had entered another hangar. According to a sign on the wall, this particular hangar was reserved for use by Fondor Spaceport Flight Control. To Mace's right, three astromech droids were jacked into a broad computer console. Rotating their domed heads, the astromechs trained their photoreceptors on the Jedi in the doorway. To Mace's left, at the far end of the hangar, several light starships rested on a landing pad. Mace spotted the FX unit carrying Princess Calvaria into one of the starships, an ion-powered Incom Corporation landing craft with a large, single-aft thrust vector.

Mace was about to run after the FX unit when he noticed a wide monitor on the console in front of the three astromechs. On the monitor, there was a digital image of the spaceport's position relative to the planet Fondor. Near the image was a numerical counter. From what he could see, there was a count-down in progress. Then he realized the awful truth: The droids had destabilized the spaceport's orbit and were deliberately steering the spaceport into Fondor's atmosphere.

As the landing craft angled for the hangar's docking port, Mace reached to his belt and removed a palm-sized tracer beacon, a device used for tracking ships across space. He whipped his arm fast, hurling the tracer straight at the landing craft. The tracer's magnetic grips sunk into the landing craft's hull, just as the vehicle blasted out of the hangar.

Mace drew his lightsaber and moved toward the three astromechs. There was a rapid series of snap-ping and clicking sounds as the droids flipped open various panels and extended weapons from their cylindrical bodies. From its domed head, one droid raised a periscope that had been modified to support a micro-laser cannon.

The astromechs fired their weapons at Mace, and his lightsaber blurred as he struck back at the fired energy bolts and slammed them back at the shooters. Despite their combined firepower, the droids were no match for the Jedi Master's skill, and all three astromechs were immediately riddled with holes made by the deftly deflected bolts. Moving in closer, Mace dragged his lightsaber in a wide arc through the droids, severing their domes from their bodies. Sparks flew from the droids, and Mace kicked them away from the computer console.

With the three astromechs defeated, Mace turned his attention to the spaceport's flight controls. He could see that the controls had been sabotaged by the rogue astromechs, but they were not beyond repair. Switching the controls over to manual, he made several adjustments until the spaceport entered a safer orbit.

Just then, the Skull Queen ran through the doorway and entered the chamber. "Where is Calvaria?" she asked. "Kit Fisto said she was captured by a droid!"

"I'll go after your daughter," Mace said. Gesturing to the fallen astromechs, he said, "These droids tried to make the spaceport fall out of orbit. Tell Kit Fisto to summon an astromech from our cruiser and make it run a complete diagnostic."

Mace knew the Skull Queen was concerned for her daughter's safety, and he expected her to protest or demand that she accompany him to pursue the droid. If necessary, he was prepared to use the Force to make her obey his command.

The Skull Queen hesitated but only for the briefest moment. "I'll tell Kit Fisto," she replied as she ran out of the hangar.

Scanning the remaining starships in the hangar, Mace was surprised to see a wedge-shaped Delta-6 starfighter in the hangar. Manufactured by Kuat Systems Engineering, the Delta-6 was a long way from the Kuat system, but it looked clean and ready to fly, and Mace was familiar with the controls. He sprinted for the starfighter, leaped into the cockpit, and lowered the canopy. Firing the engines, he zoomed out of the hangar and into space. Seconds later, the Delta-6's navigational sensor had a lock on the tracer Mace had attached to the droid's landing craft.

The Delta-6 was significantly faster than the Incom landing craft, and Mace was soon looking at the droid's vessel through his transparisteel canopy. The landing craft was heading for a ship with an unusually colorful exterior and enormous, decorative fins. Mace generally thought of starships for their utility, but as he looked at the one that the landing craft was approaching, he could only describe it as truly hideous.

Mace accelerated after the droid's ship.

CHAPTER EIGHT

Inside the main cabin of Groodo's starship, Hurlo Holowan was busily using her remote control device to make the FX unit steer the escaped landing craft. She was also fielding questions.

"When will the landing craft get here?" Senator Rodd asked.

"Soon," Holowan replied.

"When will the spaceport reach Fondor's atmosphere?" Groodo asked.

"Soon," Holowan answered.

Groodo's son, Boonda, yawned as he slithered into the cabin. He'd been taking a nap and there was spittle at the edges of his mouth. Boonda asked, "Are we home yet?"

"*Soon*," Holowan said, just to shut him up.

Boonda licked his lips as he sighted a fast-moving object through the cabin's viewport. "Hey, what kind of starfighter is that?"

"What starfighter?" Holowan asked.

"The one that's following that ion-powered Incom Corporation landing craft," Boonda responded.

Holowan cursed, "Oh, stang! There's probably a Jedi piloting that thing." She turned to Groodo and said, "In my humble opinion, the princess has just become more trouble than she's worth."

Groodo sighed. "Change of plans. Ditch the landing craft. Then get us out of here."

* * *

From his starfighter, Mace Windu watched as the Incom landing craft suddenly veered away from the hideous-looking starship and curved back toward the spaceport. He tightened his grip on the starfighter's controls and steered after the elusive droid.

As the landing craft raced closer to the spaceport, it angled for the hangar from which the droid exited. The landing craft did not decrease speed. Although Mace could only imagine the FX unit's sinister motivations, he realized the droid was attempting to crash its ship.

The Delta-6 was equipped with two dual laser cannons. Desperate to save Princess Calvaria, Mace aimed the starfighter's cannons at the landing craft's aft-thrust vector and fired.

The landing craft's thrust vector exploded. Mace had successfully disabled the ship's thruster, but because the vacuum of space offered no resistance, the landing craft continued on its collision course with the spaceport.

Mace accelerated. Bringing the Delta-6 over the landing craft, he matched the vehicle's velocity, then dipped his fighter's nose down. There was a loud *whump* as the Delta-6 made contact with the landing craft's roof, then Mace deployed the starfighter's landing gear. Equipped with claw-like grippers for zero-gravity docking, the Delta-6's landing gear latched onto the hull of the droid-piloted vehicle.

Mace hit the Delta-6's inertial dampers, and both vehicles, traveling as one, rapidly decelerated. With his starfighter still securely locked to the top of the landing craft, Mace steered into the hangar reserved for Fondor Spaceport Flight Control, and set the Incom ship down on the hangar's landing pad.

Popping the Delta-6's canopy, Mace leaped out of the starfighter's cockpit and activated his lightsaber in midair. He had expected the FX unit would put up one last fight, but as he looked through the landing craft's viewport, he saw the droid leaning at an odd angle in the cockpit. The droid's visual sensors were not illuminated, and it appeared to be shut down.

The landing craft's egress hatch was locked. Mace drove his lightsaber through the hatch and made a large, circular cut. A split second after the hatch fell away from the craft and landed on the floor, Mace was inside the vehicle.

Princess Calvaria lay motionless on a long seat. Mace touched her wrist and felt her steady pulse.

Calvaria was going to be just fine.

At this point, readers who chose to follow the adventure in the Star Wars Adventures Game Book can return to the novel *The Hostage Princess*.

CHAPTER NINE

When Princess Calvaria awoke, she was lying in her bedroom at the fortress on Nallastia. Her mother, seated on a chair beside the bed, was holding Calvaria's hand and gave it a squeeze.

"Good morning, Calvaria," the Skull Queen said. "You gave us all quite a scare."

"What happened?" Calvaria asked. "The droids on the spaceport—?"

"The droids were all destroyed," the Skull Queen said. "Except for a few bumps and bruises, no one was harmed."

Calvaria thought of Rench, then felt her blood go cold. "Mother?" she said weakly. "What day is it?"

The Skull Queen looked out the window and said, "Well, I *believe* it is still your wedding day."

"But, Mother, I don't love Prince Alto!"

"Now, now," the Skull Queen interrupted, turning to face her daughter. "Given all the excitement of the past several hours, I will allow you to reschedule your wedding, if you wish."

"Reschedule?" snapped Calvaria. "But I want to cancel it!"

The Skull Queen smiled. "Let's not be too hasty. While you're thinking about it, there's a young man who would like a word with you. He's very concerned."

Calvaria sat up in bed. "Who is it?"

"One moment." The Skull Queen rose from the chair, went to the door, and opened it. "You may come in now."

Seeing the man appear in the doorway, Calvaria's eyes went wide and her heart raced. "Rench!" she cried.

The Skull Queen looked sternly at the man, still dressed in his grease-stained coveralls, and said, "You may have five minutes with my daughter. Then she needs to rest."

The man bowed and said, "Thank you, Your Highness."

Much to Calvaria's astonishment, the Skull Queen left the room. "Oh, Rench!" the princess sighed as she gestured to the chair beside her bed, motioning him to sit beside her. "I feared you were dead!"

Seating himself, the man replied, "Woke up with a headache, that's all." He gulped nervously. Then, with an apologetic expression, he added, "Klara...I mean, *Calvaria*...I had no idea you were the Skull Queen's daughter."

Calvaria frowned. "Does this change your feelings for me?"

"No, not at all!"

"It does not bother you that I lied about my identity?"

He shook his head and patted her hand. "Am I wrong to assume you only hoped I'd fall in love with you for *you*, and not because you are a princess?"

Calvaria nodded, beaming. "Yes, that's the only reason I lied. Can you forgive me?"

"Of course. If you can forgive me, too. You see, I think I understand your situation too well. My name isn't really Rench."

Calvaria's smile froze. *"What?"*

"I'm Prince Alto of the Raptor Clan."

"Oh!" Calvaria said. "Oh, my!" Then she pushed Prince Alto off the chair and shouted, "Get out of my room at once!"

Stunned and sprawling on the floor, Alto looked up and said, "But...I thought you would forgive me, too."

"Yes, I forgive you!" Calvaria snapped. "But didn't anyone ever tell you it's bad luck for the groom to see the bride before the wedding? Now get out of here, and put on some decent clothes!"

At the landing field beside the Skull Queen's fortress, Anakin stood beside the Republic Cruiser's landing ramp and waited for Obi-Wan. After returning the Skull Queen, Princess Calvaria, and Prince Alto to Nallastia, all the Jedi had rested for the remainder of the night. As usual, Anakin had not rested well.

He looked up to the vast, blue sky. There wasn't a cloud in sight. When he'd been a child on Tatooine, he had always preferred a star-filled sky to daylight, but not just because it was cooler in the evening. The sight of the stars had filled him with hope that he would someday leave Tatooine and travel to faraway planets. And now here he was, standing on a faraway planet, his childhood dream come true. Yet instead of feeling powerful and free, he mostly felt alone.

Anakin was relieved that the stars were not visible in the Nallastian sky. If they had been, his eyes would have located the Tatooine system and he would have wondered about his mother. And then he would have looked to the Naboo system and wondered about Padmé Amidala. To make matters worse, he would not even have been looking at the starlight that he remembered, but at ancient starlight that had taken thousands of years to travel all the way to Nallastia. It made him sick to think that both Tatooine and Naboo were merely several hours away by hyperspace, yet he couldn't go to either world unless he were sent there on a mission. Although he knew he had greater freedom than others, he sometimes felt as enslaved by the Jedi Order as he had once been by Watto, the junk dealer.

Obi-Wan is holding me back, he thought with resentment. *It's not fair!*

Lowering his gaze, Anakin saw Obi-Wan and the Skull Queen approaching from the fortress. When they reached Anakin's position, he bowed, then said, "Master Windu and Kit Fisto are already on the cruiser, preparing for their return to Coruscant."

"Very good," Obi-Wan said.

"Good-bye, Anakin Skywalker," said the Skull Queen.

"Good-bye, Your Highness," said Anakin.

Obi-Wan and the Skull Queen looked at each other, then Obi-Wan turned to Anakin and said, "I'll be on board in a moment."

Anakin looked from Obi-Wan to the Skull Queen, then said, "Oh. Yes, Master." He turned and walked up the landing ramp.

The Skull Queen smiled. "Thank you for all your help, Obi-Wan."

Obi-Wan replied, "I wish we could have done more. I regret we may never find out who sent the droids to the Fondor system. But Bultar Swan will remain on Fondor Spaceport until the new security system is installed."

"Fondor Spaceport was long overdue for a new security system anyway," the Skull Queen said. "We'll have a lot of work to do here, too. I want to protect my world, yet also have outlanders feel welcome on Nallastian soil."

"Any immediate plans?"

The Skull Queen shrugged. "I thought I'd start by finding a way to shut down the force field between the Trinity Stones, and then return the power gems to the Cavern of Screaming Skulls."

"Sounds like a good start," Obi-Wan commented. He turned for one more look at the fortress, then added, "And perhaps Princess Calvaria's marriage to Prince Alto will help strengthen the ties between the Nallastian clans."

"Are you sure you can't stay for the royal wedding?"

"I'm afraid not," Obi-Wan replied, turning back to face the Skull Queen. "I am needed elsewhere."

The Skull Queen bowed her head and looked at Obi-Wan's boots. In a low voice, almost a whisper, she said, "And here."

Obi-Wan reached out to place his fingers under the Skull Queen's chin, and he gently raised her head up so her eyes met his. "I'm sorry," he said. "I really don't know what to say."

"Then don't say anything," said the Skull Queen. "Just come back to me one day."

Obi-Wan's protest was silenced by an unexpected kiss from the Skull Queen. Then, as suddenly as the kiss had been given, the Skull Queen pulled away from Obi-Wan. Before Obi-Wan could speak, the Skull Queen turned and walked off the landing field, heading for her fortress. She did not look back.

Obi-Wan boarded the Republic Cruiser. The cruiser lifted from the landing field, blasted off into the sky, and was gone.

EPILOGUE

Three days later, on the planet Coruscant, a hunched, hooded figure stepped out onto the balcony of a derelict tower to face Galactic City. Night had fallen, but the densely clustered skyscrapers appeared to shimmer in the darkness under the endlessly flowing, crowded lanes of air traffic.

From an open door behind the hooded figure, a deep voice said, "Good evening, Master Sidious." The voice belonged to a former Jedi Master, a tall, dignified man with perfectly trimmed silver hair. A black cape was clipped to his neck by a silver chain, and his tailored uniform was made of the finest materials. As a Jedi, he had been known as Count Dooku, but to his present Master, the Sith Lord Darth Sidious, he went by another name.

"Lord Tyranus," Darth Sidious replied without turning to face his apprentice. Three days earlier, when he had first heard the reports of renegade droids and exploding starships in the Fondor system, he had asked Count Dooku to investigate. Now, Darth Sidious asked, "What news from Fondor?"

The actual procedure of Count Dooku's investigation had been both dangerous and laborious, requiring him to send agents to secretly infiltrate Fondor Spaceport, access the station's extensive flight logs and security records, then follow leads and search for clues without being detected. The scattered clues included the unscheduled arrival and quick departure of an extremely gaudy starship from the planet Esseles, a security holotape that showed a hooded figure's rendezvous with the same gaudy starship, and the collected remains of several damaged droids. But despite his remarkable efforts, Dooku knew that his Master was not interested in the procedure of his investigation, only in his findings. So in a confident baritone, Dooku replied, "Groodo the Hutt, a starship manufacturer from Esseles, attempted to ruin the starship yards of Fondor. I must surmise his motive was to gain Fondor's lost business. Groodo's scheme was foiled by the Jedi, but he has so far managed to elude their suspicion. The Jedi do not know of his involvement."

Darth Sidious scowled. "Had the Hutt's scheme succeeded, it would have been a most inconvenient setback to our future plans for Fondor. Did he have accomplices?"

Darth Sidious nodded. "Evidently, there were two. The first was a droid-engineer named Hurlo Holowan. The second was..." Count Dooku could not resist a brief, dramatic pause before he finished, "Senator Rodd of Fondor."

"*Rodd*," Darth Sidious snarled. "No doubt motivated by the Hutt's money."

"Indubitably," Dooku agreed. "I must say, they all did an excellent job of avoiding detection. Like Groodo, the Senator and droid-engineer are not even suspects in the Fondor incident."

"Despite their failure to carry out their scheme, their stealth is admirable," Darth Sidious admitted. "However, we cannot allow them to interfere with our plans again. The Hutt and his cohorts must be dealt with accordingly. Contact the bounty hunter."

Count Dooku smiled. "As you wish, my Master."

NEXT ADVENTURE:
JANGO FETT VS. THE RAZOR EATERS